Copyright © 2001 by NordSüd Verlag AG, CH-8005 Zürich, Switzerland.
First published in Switzerland under the title *Frohe Ostern! Pauli.*
English text copyright © 2001 by NorthSouth Books Inc., New York 10016.
Translated by Rosemary Lanning.

First published in the United States, Great Britain, Canada, Australia, and New Zealand
in 2001, 2014 by NorthSouth Books, Inc., an imprint of NordSüd Verlag AG, CH-8005
Zürich, Switzerland.

Distributed in the United States by NorthSouth Books Inc., New York 10016.
Library of Congress Cataloging-in-Publication Data is available.
ISBN: 978-0-7358-4161-1 (trade edition)
1 3 5 7 9 • 10 8 6 4 2
Printed in Germany by Grafisches Centrum Cuno GmbH & Co. KG,
39240 Calbe, January 2014.
www.northsouth.com

FSC
www.fsc.org
MIX
Paper from
responsible sources
FSC® C043106

Brigitte Weninger
Eve Tharlet

# Happy Easter, Davy!

Translated by Rosemary Lanning

North
South

Spring had come at last!
Davy, the little rabbit, and his family
sat outside their burrow, soaking up
the warm sunshine.

Suddenly, Davy's big brother Max
came running.

"Guess what I just heard," said Max excitedly. "Tomorrow is Easter, when children get presents and pretty eggs. A rabbit called the Easter Bunny brings them, and I heard that he lives right here in this wood!"

"Where?" asked Davy.

Father Rabbit scratched his head and said, "There are lots of rabbits in the wood, but I've never met the Easter Bunny."

"Presents!" squeaked baby Mia.

"I want a present too!" said big sister Lina.

"Why doesn't he bring *us* anything?"

"Let's go ask him," said Manni.

So off they went to find the Easter Bunny.

They searched high and low,
but the Easter Bunny was
nowhere to be found.

Davy's brothers and sisters went home disappointed,
but Davy stayed behind to think.

"It's not fair," he said to Nicky, his toy rabbit.
"The Easter Bunny should visit us. We're bunnies!"

Suddenly Davy jumped up.
"I have an idea!" he said.
"Come on, Nicky. We've
got work to do."

"First we need some eggs," said Davy.
He saw a nest with five speckled eggs, but
he couldn't take those. They had baby birds
inside, waiting to hatch.
Davy ran down to the river and found
some beautiful, egg-shaped pebbles instead.
"Now for the presents!"

Davy found a secret place
to work all day long.

First he painted the pebbles.
Then he made a basket for
Lina, a doll for Mia, and boats
for Max and Manni.

"Finished at last!" he said.
"Tomorrow everyone will
think the Easter Bunny
came after all!"

That night Davy was so excited he could hardly sleep. When dawn broke, he tiptoed outside and hid the eggs and presents. His brothers and sisters were still fast asleep when he crept back into bed.

At last the bunnies woke up and hopped out of the burrow.

Lina tripped over something round.

"Look! I've found an Easter egg!" she cried.

"And here's another one!" said Max. "The Easter Bunny did come!"

Lina, Manni, Mia, and Max started an egg hunt. They were so excited when they found all the other eggs—and the presents!

"What about you, Davy?" said Mother Rabbit. "Didn't you find anything?"

Davy blushed from head to toe.

Now they would guess that he was the Easter Bunny!

"N-n-not yet," he stammered.

Father Rabbit watched patiently
as Davy looked around.

Davy couldn't believe his eyes! He found
a pretty painted egg and a little wooden
flute. Who could have hidden them?

Father Rabbit said, "It looks like the kind
Easter Bunny brought something for all
our children! This calls for a celebration!"

So the Rabbit family
had a happy Easter
picnic out in the meadow.
And the happiest of
all was Davy, the
secret Easter Bunny!